Sir Gadabout
and the Little Horror

Find out more about *Sir Gadabout* at
http://mysite.freeserve.com/gadabout

Martyn Beardsley

* * * * * * * * * * *

Sir Gadabout

and the Little Horror

Illustrated by Tony Ross

Orion
Children's Books

First published in Great Britain in 2002
as a Dolphin Paperback
by Orion Children's Books
Reissued 2006 by Orion Children's Books
a division of the Orion Publishing Group Ltd
Orion House
5 Upper St Martin's Lane
London WC2H 9EA

1 3 5 7 9 10 8 6 4 2

The Orion Publishing Group's policy is to use papers that are natural,
renewable and recyclable products and made from wood grown in sustainable
forests. The logging and manufacturing processes are expected to conform to
the environmental regulations of the country of origin.

A catalogue record for this book
is available from the British Library

Printed in Great Britain by Clays Ltd, St Ives plc

ISBN-10 1 85881 893 1
ISBN-13 978 1 85881 893 1

www.orionbooks.co.uk

for Heather and Philip

Contents

1

Castle Stonefist

A long, long time ago, well before anyone had won the top prize on *Who Wants to be a Millionaire?* there was a castle called Soggysocks. This was a very unusual name for a castle, but then it was a very unusual castle. The knights who lived there took in washing and ironing from villages far and wide, and generally very little else happened there. Some knights became so bored that they fell asleep standing up.

This would make an extremely dull story — but fortunately, not far from the castle called Soggysocks was another one called Camelot. This was a magnificent building whose stout walls kept out all invaders (except the knights of Soggysocks who came to collect Camelot's dirty clothes every fortnight).

The famous King Arthur lived in Camelot. He was a well-loved king and a powerful warrior, but he never had quite as much laundry as the other knights because he had dry skin and didn't sweat very much. Also, the T-shirts he wore on, say, Wednesday, he tended to wear again as a vest on Thursday. This didn't always go down well with his beautiful wife Guinevere, who would have preferred him to wear a clean T-shirt every day. However, she was so busy making ironing-boards for the knights of Soggysocks that she never had time to check on King Arthur's underwear.

But this story doesn't start at Camelot — nor even at Soggysocks, though the knights there had just received an exciting consignment of laundry from a famous celebrity. (I'm not allowed to say who, and anyway it was long before she married David Beckham.)

Where was I? Oh, yes: this story begins at the gates of Castle Stonefist, many days ride to the north of Camelot. Here waited Sir Percy, King Arthur's calmest, cleverest, most polite knight. He never lost his temper. And because of this King Arthur had chosen him for a special mission, which is why he was waiting at Castle Stonefist, where he would have to deal with Lord Stonefist, a powerful baron with a large army. Lord Stonefist had once been at war with King Arthur, and even came close to winning. Things had been rather tricky between them ever since, so Guinevere came up with the idea of allowing Lord Stonefist's young son to come to Camelot for extra-special training with the famous knights of the Round Table.

Sir Percy had the skills to ensure that nothing would go wrong during the talks with Lord Stonefist (who had a bit of a temper) and that his son would be safely delivered to Camelot. With Sir Percy was another

knight who did not have quite so many skills.
In fact some said he had no skills at all, and
most said he was the Worst Knight in the
World. This was, of course, Sir Gadabout,
who had been sent along because ... well,
King Arthur could think of nothing else to
do with him.

Sir Gadabout was wearing a brand-new
suit of armour which Guinevere had made
from wood left over from a new batch of
ironing-boards she had been working on.
(Those were cleverly made in the actual

shape of a shirt, so that you could iron it all in one go and didn't have to fiddle about with it and end up forgetting which sleeve you had done.) Because it was a hot summer, Guinevere had fastened the pieces of Sir Gadabout's armour loosely together with leather straps to let more air in. As Sir Gadabout trotted along on his horse, the pieces of wood jangled together and he sounded rather like a wind-chime, which kept everyone amused on the long journey north. For a while.

With Sir Gadabout were his usual helpers. Herbert was his squire, or personal attendant. He was young, short and stocky and incredibly loyal to his master through thick and thin. Travelling inside Herbert's saddlebag was a rather overweight ginger cat called Sidney Smith. He wasn't incredibly loyal either to Sir Gadabout or Herbert. He knew what they were like, and just came along for a laugh.

But he was useful to them in one way, because Sidney Smith was no ordinary, overweight ginger moggy; he happened to be the cat of the great wizard Merlin. On this occasion Merlin had taught them a spell in case they got fed up with the long, slow journey and wanted to get it over with quickly. All they had to do was chant the magic words, and their horses would go ten times faster without getting tired!

Sir Gadabout had been very excited about the spell, and had been asking to use it ever since they had left Camelot. Even though his new horse, Buck, was much faster than his poor old one (though a lot more temperamental) the spell would give him the chance to ride faster than anyone had *ever* ridden! But Merlin had told them it could only be

used once, and as it was such lovely weather and there was no hurry, the others wanted to take their time (despite the wind-chimes). Sir Percy, who was in charge of the expedition, told Sir Gadabout he would have to wait till the return journey. But being the clever knight he was, he said it in such a way as to make Sir Gadabout think he was getting his own way. This was exactly why Sir Percy had been chosen to deal with Lord Stonefist, with his very short temper and very large army. Goodness knows what would happen if the meeting had been left in Sir Gadabout's hands ...

So there they were, outside the gates of the castle, preparing to collect Lord Stonefist's son.

"Now, leave all the talking to me," said Sir Percy. "After all," he added, seeing Sir Gadabout's disappointed look, "we have to keep up your reputation as the strong, silent type!"

"What about his reputation as the biggest bungler in armour?" queried Sidney Smith. Herbert pressed the cat's head into the saddle-bag and fastened the strap.

"*Strong silent type!*" Sir Gadabout repeated proudly to himself. "Very well. But can I say the 'Ten Times Faster' spell when we go home?"

"Certainly," said Sir Percy.

Sir Gadabout and Herbert dismounted and took a drink from their flasks. Hearing the trickling water, Sidney Smith managed to squeeze out of the saddlebag and join them.

"Oh dear …" exclaimed Sir Gadabout suddenly. "I think I've forgotten the spell!"

Herbert scratched his head. "I think it starts: *Horse so strong …*"

"That's it!" agreed Sir Gadabout. "*Horse so strong, I am your master …*"

"I really don't think you should carry on!" warned Sidney Smith.

But Sir Gadabout was too excited to listen. "*Hear these words and go TEN TIMES FASTER!*"

"WHOAAAAAAAH!!!" shrieked Sir Percy.

If his horse had been fired from a cannon it could hardly have taken off more violently.

His cry faded as he disappeared in a blur over a distant hill. All that could be seen was a trail of dust where he had been.

"Whoops," said Sir Gadabout.

"He sounded a bit upset, sire," commented Herbert.

"With a touch of panic thrown in," added Sidney Smith.

"Funny," said Sir Gadabout. "He always seemed such a calm fellow …"

They all stood looking at the long trail of dust as it settled gradually into the shimmering earth. Then they turned to look at the formidable walls of Castle Stonefist. Then they looked back at the horizon.

"He'll probably be back in a minute," said Sir Gadabout hopefully.

2

Later

"He'll probably be back in a day or two," said Sir Gadabout as they woke, stretching and yawning next day ...

3

Much Later

"I don't think he's coming back," said Sir
Gadabout at the end of the week ...

4

Later Still

"We're kippered," grumbled Sidney Smith, surveying the Sir Percyless horizon.

"It looks like someone else will have to deal with the terrible and powerful Lord Stonefist," Sir Gadabout admitted. "Er, why is everyone looking at me?"

In fact, Sir Percy's horse had neither stopped nor slowed down till reaching Camelot, hundreds of miles away. All Sir Percy's fillings had dropped out, and he had to have a very powerful ointment applied to his bottom three times a day for the next six weeks.

"I heard that Lord Stonefist once turned a man completely inside out with his bare hands just for coughing too loudly," fibbed Sidney Smith mischievously.

Sir Gadabout coughed. He couldn't help

himself. And then he began to shake so much that his wooden armour played what sounded like a snappy Irish jig.

"I also heard," said the cat with a mean chuckle, "that he once declared war on Prussia because someone put one sugar in his tea instead of two. And he wasn't even a Prussian!"

Sir Gadabout gulped.

"I don't believe a word of it!" cried Herbert. Funnily enough this last tale was true, although Sidney Smith wasn't to know that.

"And he *hates* wind chimes!" continued Sidney Smith, enjoying himself.

Sir Gadabout made a whimpering noise like a hungry guinea-pig.

And so the three of them nervously approached the dark, gigantic gates of Castle Stonefist. Herbert and Sidney Smith secretly feared for what might happen if by some strange chance Sir Gadabout should upset Lord Stonefist. Well, actually Herbert feared this secretly. Sidney Smith declared, "The fool's going to start a *war*. That's a first even for us."

Sir Gadabout himself was walking in a

strangely slow and stiff manner, trying not to sound like a wind-chime. And he could be heard muttering, "*Two sugars not one ... Two sugars not one ...*"

5

Little Roger

Later that day, Sir Gadabout, Herbert and Sidney Smith found themselves in a large room inside Castle Stonefist. Lord Stonefist had been keeping them waiting for two hours already. The rumour was that one of his knights had burped during breakfast, and the baron was at that moment dangling the unfortunate culprit over the castle battlements by the ankles and lecturing him about unpleasant noises at the breakfast table. On hearing this, Sir Gadabout took to standing rigidly like a statue, even more terrified of the wind-chime sounds his armour made.

Just when they were beginning to get extremely bored, the door opened and a small boy struggled in dragging a large wooden, jewel-encrusted chest. Once the chest was inside the room, the boy closed the door and

looked at them all solemnly. He had big, honest-looking blue eyes, neatly combed hair and was smartly dressed.

"I am Roger, Lord Stonefist's squire. I'm sorry to have to tell you that my master has run away with the Queen of Gargantua and won't be coming back ever, so you might as well all go home. But before he went he asked me to divide some of his riches between you to make up for your wasted journey."

He opened the lid of the chest, and his face was lit up by the sun reflecting off the many wonderful treasures inside. "Take whatever you want," added Roger, "but be quick and then leave immediately. The, er, Inspector of Castles says the walls are in a bad condition and liable to fall down at any moment."

And with that, he disappeared. Sir Gadabout and the others were shocked at this news – but the precious goods in the chest managed to take their minds off it. Herbert was soon wearing a tunic that was far too big for him, made of the finest silk embroidered with gold, and he had various pieces of price-less jewellery to take home to his mum (or so he claimed). Sidney Smith had a feeling there was something fishy about the boy's story – but he wasn't complaining as he had found a solid silver dish with diamonds around the rim. He thought it would make a marvellous Sunday-best milk dish.

Sir Gadabout, meanwhile, was brandishing a magnificent sword which had jewels in the hilt and diamonds set along the gleaming, razor-sharp blade. It was almost as impressive as King Arthur's famous Excalibur. *And* there was a matching shield.

"We'd better go now, sire," said Herbert at last, glancing nervously at the walls around them.

At first, Sir Gadabout was in no hurry. By now, he was in the middle of a fight with an imaginary enemy (but not doing very well – Sir Gadabout even lost imaginary fights). But a deep, heavy rumbling sound made them all stop and look around. It sounded like the walls were coming down already.

"Quick! Head for the hills!" cried Sir Gadabout in a panic.

The heavy rumbling was in fact nothing to do with the castle walls (which were as strong and firm as could be) but was the sound of Lord Stonefist approaching very quickly, and in a *very* bad mood (he was always in a bad mood, but when he was in a *very* bad mood you had to look out).

The door burst open, and there stood a tall figure with a broad chest and muscular arms. And that was only Lord Stonefist's little brother Ernie. When the baron himself came in, he was even bigger. He was dressed all in black, with a great cloak that swirled about him like the wings of a gigantic bird of prey, and black gauntlets with sharp silver studs sticking out of them. (He found these useful for punching holes in paper; that way he didn't have to use one of those little machines that always get jammed.)

Lord Stonefist stood in the doorway, blocking out the light and casting a shadow over the three visitors. He slowly raised a hand and pointed a studded finger right at Sir Gadabout.

"He's got me sword! Me precious *Lightning Strike!*" gasped Lord Stonefist. He had a curiously high-pitched voice that sounded as though it was on the verge of tears.

"No wonder he's heading for the hills," muttered Ernie.

Sir Gadabout tried to explain, but no sensible words would come out (not that they often did). "N-n-n-not stealing ... walls ... Queen of Gargantua ... wind-chimes crumbling ..." He was trembling so much that his armour sounded more like a machine-gun than wind-chimes, and splinters flew around the room so that everyone had to keep ducking.

Lord Stonefist's pointing finger moved to Herbert. "Me best tunic! Me wife's finest jewels!"

"Hanging's too good for 'em," Ernie whined.

"Find a cat! Any cat! Chop its tail and ears

off!" wailed the baron.

"That'll make you feel better," Ernie whispered soothingly. "For a start!"

"Yes, sire," said a guard standing beside Lord Stonefist. But before he could do anything, Ernie had spotted Sidney Smith.

"Cat! He'll do!"

The guard advanced on Sidney Smith, drawing a sharp knife from his belt.

"Now, look here my good man," said the cat in a stern voice he had picked up from Merlin. The guard was so surprised to hear a ginger cat talking that he did stop.

"This is all a misunderstanding," Sidney Smith explained. "We were told that you had run away with the Queen of Gargantua ..."

"WHAT?!" cried Lord Stonefist.

"Such lies," hissed Ernie into his brother's ear. "Such a virtuous lady!"

"And," continued Sidney Smith, "that we could take what we wanted if we left quickly because the castle is about to fall down. So there!"

"FALL DOWN?!" shrieked Lord Stonefist.

"Vile insult," murmured Ernie. "Finest castle in the north."

Lord Stonefist took a step closer to them.

So did Ernie. "Before I kill you all slowly and painfully, pray tell me – WHY?" His squeaky, high voice started to sound weepy. "*Why spoil my day?*" His eyes began to water. "Why ruin my life?" His bottom lip began to tremble. "Why steal my –" and then it all became too much for him, and he turned his back on them and began to blub like a baby. "*I'm not crying!*" he sobbed, his cloak wrapped round his head.

"Not crying," added Ernie. "Fly in his eye – you all saw it. Lord Stonefist *never* cries, never mind what anyone might tell you."

"It was HIM!" shouted Herbert suddenly. He had just noticed Roger lurking in the doorway. "He told us all the lies!"

"*I never!*" replied Roger sweetly and innocently.

"You little horror!" Sidney Smith accused.

"*Now they accuse my only son!*" wailed Lord Stonefist into his cloak.

"But that's your squire," said Sir Gadabout.

Ernie shook his head. "His only son. A sweet son. A perfect, well-mannered son. Little horror indeed."

"*Cut things off them!*" blubbed Lord Stonefist. "*Stick things into them — long, sharp things.*"

"I've had enough of this," Sidney Smith declared. He had just remembered a spell he'd seen Merlin perform. "*Forget my name ...*" he began chanting.

"Eh?" said Lord Stonefist.

"*Forget my face ...*"

"What?" queried Ernie.

"*Forget we met, and begin again!*"

"Umm — who are these people?" Lord Stonefist asked.

Sidney Smith finished the spell:

"Dry those tears,
Downcast chappie,
Lose that frown
And BE HAPPY!"

An amazing change came over Lord
Stonefist. The spell was so powerful that his
tears dried up and his face brightened as if lit
by a sunbeam. He began to giggle like a little
boy being tickled. "Ah!" he chortled. "You
must be the visitors from Camelot. Look after
young Roger for us, won't you. Though you
won't have any trouble – he's a little angel!"

"A little cherub!" tittered Ernie.

Sir Gadabout froze on the spot as Lord Stonefist pinched one of his cheeks and Ernie teasingly kissed him on the other. "Er ... c-can someone explain ..." he stammered.

"Later. *The spell soon wears off,*" said Sidney Smith, trying to hurry their exit from Castle Stonefist with sweet little Roger.

"Have a safe journey!" Lord Stonefist called as they departed.

"A pleasant one!" added Ernie brightly.

Still Sir Gadabout hesitated, scratching his helmet and trying to figure things out.

"*GO!*" cried Sidney Smith. "The spell is wearing off!"

Lord Stonefist suddenly gave his head a shake and rubbed his eyes. He saw before him the people he had caught stealing his sword and valuables. A dark expression came over his face. "And tell King Arthur ... tell him ... THIS MEANS *WAR!*" he whined, and promptly burst into tears.

"And Lord Stonefist's been peeling an onion, so don't start any rumours!" shouted Ernie as Sir Gadabout and Co. galloped away.

6

The Joke Turns Sour

"Now, my boy," said Sir Gadabout as they began the long ride south. "What kind of things do you like to do?"

Roger smiled sweetly at Sir Gadabout. "Flower arranging, sir, and helping people, and skipping!"

"Skipping the truth, more like," remarked Sidney Smith, who had recognised the little horror for what he was.

"Please keep that horrid cat away from me, sir," Roger pleaded. "I'm afraid I might catch fleas!"

Sidney Smith growled like a Staffordshire bull terrier.

It was another hot day, and when they reached a river of cool, sparkling water, they stopped for a drink. Not long after setting off again, Sir Gadabout was heard to say,

"Goodness me – the world is turning upside down!"

When they looked at him, his saddle was gradually slipping down Buck's side, and Sir Gadabout was going with it. Finally, he was hanging upside down.

"Something is definitely not right here," he commented as his head bumped along the ground.

They discovered that his saddle had been deliberately loosened during their stop by the river.

"It was him!" accused Roger, pointing at Sidney Smith.

Although Sidney denied it, he *had* played tricks on them in the past, and Sir Gadabout gave him a suspicious look before they set off again.

They had arranged to spend the night at the castle of a friend of King Arthur's – Sir Pelligrew the Portly – and they arrived there just as it was beginning to grow dark.

"Welcome, welcome!" chuckled Sir Pelligrew the Portly, who was, well, *portly*. "I want to have the grass in my garden washed – do you know where I should take it?"

Sir Gadabout was perplexed by this question. "I, er, I'm not quite sure."

"Why, I think I shall take it to the laundry! *Lawn-dree* – get it?"

Herbert laughed so much that he was rolling on the floor kicking his legs in the air. Only Sir Pelligrew himself, whose laugh seemed to echo around inside his huge belly then erupt into the air like a hurricane, laughed louder. Sidney Smith sniffed (which you will find is a bit of a tongue-twister if you try to say it quickly) and said he'd seen better jokes on ice-lolly sticks.

Sir Gadabout simply didn't get it. "But if you take your grass to the laundry, won't all the bits get stuck inside the machine ..."

This made Sir Pelligrew laugh even louder, and all the candles in the hall they had entered blew out, and servants had to come rushing in to light them again (it seemed as though they had had plenty of practice at this).

"King Arthur is a very, very good friend of mine, and I'm putting you in my finest guest rooms," said Sir Pelligrew once he had got his breath back from all the laughing. He and King Arthur had become very good friends ever since the king had actually laughed his

36

socks off at one of Sir Pelligrew's corniest jokes.

Sir Pelligrew the Portly took them along a corridor until they came to the third door on the left, which he threw open. When Sir Gadabout, Herbert and Sidney Smith went inside they found it was a lovely, cosy room, with comfortable beds and beautiful decorations. No one noticed that Roger was still hanging around suspiciously outside.

"Now," said Sir Pelligrew, "you will make sure you have a pencil with you, won't you."

"A pencil?" repeated Sir Gadabout.

"Well," chortled Sir Pelligrew, "you'll need

something to *draw* the curtains with, won't you?!" Unfortunately he laughed so much that he blew the curtains down. However, a team of servants scurried in immediately and replaced them, just as if they were used to doing it all the time.

Herbert laughed until he cried. Sir Gadabout couldn't figure it out, since the servants had just drawn the curtains ... Sidney Smith groaned, "Close the door, quick – I can't stand many more jokes like this."

"Ah! A little pussy!" exclaimed Sir

Pelligrew, noticing Sidney Smith for the first time.

Sidney Smith's tail waved in the air and the fur bristled on his back – he hated being called that.

Sir Pelligrew pretended to whisper something to Sir Gadabout, though he was saying it loud enough for them all to hear. "I never trust cats with anything important myself..."

"And why not?" Sidney Smith demanded.

"Because they always get in a FLAP!"

Sidney Smith didn't reply, he simply slammed the door in Sir Pelligrew the Portly's face – but his laughter blew it wide open again, making him roar like an elephant being tickled.

"I wouldn't say cats get in a flap especially," mused Sir Gadabout, looking very puzzled. "Sometimes dogs get a bit excited, but –"

"What's the difference," interrupted Sidney Smith irritably, "between an astronaut and Sir Gadabout?"

"I don't know," Herbert replied.

"One's got his head in space, the other's got lots of space in his head."

"Er, which one's which?" Sir Gadabout asked.

Roger met Sir Pelligrew the Portly outside. He had a plan. He lived a very lazy, spoiled life at Castle Stonefist, and had no desire to go through all the years of hard work involved in becoming a knight of the Round Table. It would be bad enough having to do all the training – but the thought of being taught by *Sir Gadabout* of all people meant that he would stoop to anything to get out of it.

"My father didn't really send me with these people," Roger claimed, making tears come into his big blue eyes as he looked imploringly at Sir Pelligrew.

"Really?"

"Oh, no. They've kidnapped me and are

going to sell me into slavery. But don't tell them I told you – Sir Gadabout said he would chop me up and feed me to his hamster if I said anything."

"Well, I never! Knights of the Round Table don't usually act like that. I'll have to think about it – I'll talk to you again in the morning. Good night, young fellow, and keep safe!"

Roger gave Sir Pelligrew a goodnight kiss on the cheek. "You remind me of my favourite uncle," he said sweetly. "Good night!"

However, a different Roger rejoined the others – the Little Horror. He assumed a very shocked expression. "I've just got a secret message from one of the servants – Sir Pelligrew plans to kidnap me!"

"Whatever for?" asked Sir Gadabout.

"Well, er, he hasn't got any children of his own, and he's afraid that when he dies there will be nobody left to go on telling all the jokes he's thought up. He's going to keep me locked in a little dark room until I've learned them all!"

"There could be no worse form of torture," Sidney Smith gasped. "But it serves you right."

Herbert didn't agree. "I'll take Roger's place," he volunteered heroically.

"No!" said Sir Gadabout. "We shall be on our guard, and slip away at first light!"

While they were asleep that night the Little Horror was busy creeping around the castle. Very early the next day, they were woken by a big commotion coming from the vicinity of Sir Pelligrew's bedroom.

Sir Pelligrew the Portly was fast asleep, snoring very loudly. When he breathed in, his large belly rose in the air like a whale leaping out of the water. When he breathed out, a feather on his face was blown three feet into the air, then floated back down again. Beside the bed was a sign:

COME AND SEE THE FAT FOOLE SNORE !!
10 p TODAY ONLY
CURTESY OF GADABOUT ENTERPRISES
(THIS MAN IS SO DAFT HE DOESN'T REELIZE WE ARE KIDNAPPING AN INNACENT LITTLE BOY)

A crowd had followed a series of similar signs from the castle gates, and were now standing around Sir Pelligrew's bed laughing and cheering at the sight before them.

At first, Sir Pelligrew dreamt that people were laughing at his jokes. But eventually the noise woke him up. He spat the feather out – and read the sign.

"So it's true! Sir Gadabout is going to kidnap Roger," he bellowed. "I must save the boy!"

Meanwhile, Sir Gadabout and Co. were hurriedly getting dressed when they heard Sir Pelligrew charging along the corridors shouting, "GET THE BOY! GET THE BOY BEFORE THEY ESCAPE!" (Fortunately for Sir Gadabout, all Sir Pelligrew's guards and servants, instead of joining the chase, were dutifully laughing and

congratulating their lord on his latest joke.)

"So it's true!" cried Sir Gadabout.

"Quick – through the window!" said Herbert.

Roger had returned to Sir Gadabout's room so that Sir Pelligrew would believe he was being kidnapped. He planned to nip into a wardrobe while they were escaping – but his pockets were now so full of the ten-pence pieces he had collected from spectators that they slowed him down. Sidney Smith, who had been keeping a close eye on him, tripped him up as he tried to put his plan into action. Herbert, thinking he had stumbled, scooped him up with his big fist and lifted him through the window.

As they galloped away, they heard Sir Pelligrew shouting, "THIS IS NO JOKE! KIDNAP! MURDER! WAR ON SIR GADABOUT AND CAMELOT!"

Sidney Smith's head came out of Herbert's saddlebag once they were in the clear. "I reckon the kid had something to do with this," he hissed.

"*I never!*" cried Roger, opening his big blue eyes wide and fluttering his eyelashes.

"Roger saved the day!" Sir Gadabout agreed. "If he hadn't told us about Sir Pelligrew's treachery, he would have been taken from us!"

Roger looked at Sidney Smith and grinned. The cat narrowed his eyes and gave him his most hateful look, then disappeared back into the saddlebag muttering horrible things.

7

The Left Against the Right

Sir Pelligrew the Portly was hardly the fastest rider in the world, and even Sir Gadabout and his companions soon managed to leave him well behind. The next few days' riding were fairly uneventful. The nights were so warm they were able to sleep out under the stars. But when dark clouds began to approach rapidly on a strong breeze, and they saw distant flashes of lightning, they decided to find shelter for the night.

They came to a crossroads with a signpost in the middle which said, *Castle Left — Right.*

"I think we ought to see if we can shelter there for the night," said Herbert, keeping an eye on the approaching thunderstorm. "But I'm not sure which way we're supposed to go ..."

Sidney Smith's head popped up and sur-

veyed the scene. "Well I think it means 'Castle
Left is to the right.' We go right."

"No, no," said Roger. "I know this area. It
means 'Castle on the left – Castle Right'."

"Oh dear," said Sir Gadabout, completely
flummoxed (which wasn't difficult for him).
"Perhaps we should go straight on."

"Nonsensical   nincompoop,"   muttered
Sidney Smith.

Sir Gadabout, by the way, was no longer
sounding like a wind-chime. He had found
some sticky tape in Herbert's saddlebag and
stuck hundreds of little bits all over his wood-
en armour to prevent the different pieces
from jangling together.

"Sir," said Roger, gazing at Sir Gadabout
with his honest blue eyes. "The left-hand

road definitely leads to Castle Right, where we are bound to find a room for the night. You are one of my favourite knights in the whole world – I have always followed your adventures, and I would never lie to you."

"*Hmmph!*" snorted Sidney Smith.

Sir Gadabout proudly stuck his chest out so much that some of the bits of sticky tape burst open. "Roger is a very clever little boy, and I believe him. We turn left!"

The left-hand road took them as far as Happy Harry's House of Hats and then came to a dead-end. Herbert did buy himself a natty bearskin – one of those big black hats that soldiers wear outside Buckingham Palace – which he thought made him look taller. But that didn't get them any closer to the castle.

"I said we should have gone right for Castle Left, sir," Roger said sadly to Sir Gadabout.

"You said left to Castle Right!" accused Sidney Smith.

"*I never*! I do believe, little pussycat, that Sir Gadabout, who has one of the most brilliant minds and memories of all the knights of the Round Table, will recall that I said 'Right for Castle Left'."

Some more bits of sticky tape popped apart on Sir Gadabout's armour. "I remember it quite clearly. If only you'd listened to him we wouldn't have wasted all this time!"

Sidney Smith was so angry – not only that they wouldn't believe him, but especially at being called a "little pussycat" – that he almost exploded there and then. He sank back inside the saddlebag and sulked for quite some time.

They found Castle Left – for that was its name on account of the fact that they only employed left-handed knights, for some rea-son that has long ago been forgotten – just as the first big drops of rain began to splatter around them, and the thunder and lightning grew closer and louder. Unfortunately, Sir

Gadabout was extremely afraid of thunder
and lightning. Every time he heard thunder,
not only did it make him jump, but he invari-
ably also waved his arms in the air and cried
out for his mother in a spookily screeching
voice.

The guards at Castle Left took them to the
room of the owner, Sir Sinistral, whose room
was the third door on the left (*all* the doors
in this castle were on the left). Sir Gadabout
explained who they were and why they were
there – in a roundabout sort of way.

"I would normally let you stay for as long as you like," said Sir Sinistral, with a worried expression. "But you have come at a difficult time. Tomorrow we are going to be attacked by the army of the treacherous Sir Dexter. The reasons are long and complicated, but needless to say this will not be a safe place to remain."

"But Sir Gadabout is one of the greatest knights in the world," said Roger. "With him you are sure to win!"

"I was going to say that," said a rather disgruntled Herbert.

"Er ... one of the *greatest* knights? But I'd heard that he was ..."

"Well, you heard wrong!" interrupted Herbert. "He *is* one of the greatest knights."

"Except Sir Lancelot," added Sidney Smith. "And Sir Bors, and Sir Gawain, and –" Sidney Smith would have gone on to reel off the names of every knight he knew had he not been stopped by Herbert shoving one of his smelly socks into the cat's mouth.

But Sir Sinistral was desperate enough for *any* help, and agreed to let them stay.

As he took them to their room, Sir Gadabout was already becoming nervous

about the battle the next day. The rain had
loosened the sticky tape on his armour,
allowing the pieces to jangle again. His trembling seemed to be causing it to play a tune
by one of those girl bands – whose name I
can't quite remember. Not only that, but the
loose bits of tape flapped and whistled
around, providing a ghostly harmony.

"Er, interesting armour you Round Table
knights have," commented Sir Sinistral as he
bade them goodnight.

Next morning Sir Gadabout and Co.
accompanied Sir Sinistral to the battlefield,
where they were confronted by Sir Dexter
and his powerful army. Black clouds hovered
overhead, and thunder and lightning filled
the air. Sir Sinistral's knights lined up on the

left, Sir Dexter's on the right. When Sir Gadabout saw the enemy, he insisted that he had forgotten to fold his pyjamas neatly before he had left, and was prevented from returning only after a desperate struggle.

Then a surprising thing happened. Sir Dexter himself rode forward alone and demanded to speak to them.

"I have heard that you have a knight of the Round Table with you – I think you must be getting desperate, Sir Sinistral."

"You'll never know how right you are," muttered Sidney Smith.

"Therefore," continued Sir Dexter, "I have

a suggestion. We are two powerful armies and a lot of blood will be shed today, whoever wins. So let us settle it by single combat. I challenge your famous knight to a duel to the death, the winner wins the war. Let ours be the only blood that is shed!"

"Sir Gadabout accepts the challenge!" Roger piped up at the top of his voice.

"*I was going to say that!*" complained Herbert. "Will you please stop doing that?"

At that moment lightning streaked through the dark sky and hit a tree, which burst into flames. At the same time, thunder made the ground shake beneath them.

Sir Gadabout's arms shot into the air like someone being held up at gunpoint. "*Mothuuuurgh!*" he screeched wildly, causing all the horses within earshot to buck and whinny frantically.

"Who or what is that?" asked Sir Dexter.

"Sir Gadabout of Camelot!" cried Herbert proudly, beating Roger to it.

Sir Dexter rode away with such a dark and evil laugh that the remaining sticky tape peeled off Sir Gadabout's armour and floated to the ground. The two knights prepared for battle.

8

The Forest of the Undead

When Sir Dexter's army saw Sir Gadabout, in his clinking-clanking armour, clumsily preparing to charge, they laughed out loud. Their own lord was bigger, stronger, and carrying the scars of many battles.

What nobody noticed was little Roger slipping away from Sir Sinistral's side and tip-toeing towards Sir Dexter's army. Nobody noticed, that is, except Sidney Smith. His sharp eyes didn't miss much, and he crept after the boy. The cat watched as Roger approached Sir Dexter's squire, and he leaned close to listen as the boy whispered something in the squire's ear.

Just as Sir Gadabout levelled his long spear and began to charge, the squire passed the whisper on to his master, and Sir Dexter suddenly turned very pale.

There was a gasp from Sir Dexter's army

as, instead of meeting Sir Gadabout head-on and knocking him into the middle of next week, Sir Dexter turned in panic and tried to escape!

Even Sir Sinistral seemed surprised, but Herbert said, "Great knights of the Round Table have this effect on the enemy, sire."

This was all especially strange as Sir Gadabout, who had long believed that the sharp points on spears were very dangerous, had covered the end of his with a large rubber ball. What only Sidney Smith knew was

that Roger had informed the squire that the thing on the end of Sir Gadabout's spear was actually a bomb!

Things began to go downhill fast.

Word in Sir Dexter's camp soon got round that they had been tricked by Sir Gadabout and his secret weapon. Sir Gadabout, who had been feeling very much the part, if somewhat surprised, as he chased the mighty Sir Dexter all over the place, suddenly saw the whole of the enemy army begin to surge towards him, crying "*TREACHERY!*"

"Er … one at a time, good knights," Sir Gadabout protested feebly.

Then, an eagle-eyed knight on Sir Sinistral's side noticed Roger standing in Sir Dexter's camp, chuckling at the mayhem he had caused. "THE BOY'S A SPY! IT'S A TRICK!"

The upshot of all this was that Sir Gadabout, Herbert, Sidney Smith and Roger found themselves being pursued through three counties by two powerful armies of angry knights.

"It's not fair!" cried Sir Gadabout as he held on to Buck's reins for dear life. "I was winning!"

"Only because the brat said you had a bomb on the end of your spear," shouted Sidney Smith above the sound of galloping hooves.

"I never!" protested Roger.

He blinked his big blue eyes at Sir Gadabout. This time, Sir Gadabout looked at him, and wondered …

Fortunately, large armies can't travel fast for long, and they were eventually left behind. *Unfortunately,* Sir Gadabout, in a moment of weakness, once more insisted that they took

the Little Horror's advice on the way to go.
The path they took led to a vast forest. There
was a sign by the side of the path where it led
into the trees:

"Ooeer!" remarked Herbert. Sidney Smith
was, unusually for him, speechless. Even
Roger looked a little pale. As for Sir
Gadabout, he had lost so many pieces of
wood from his armour during the headlong
flight from the two armies that he was down

to his Butterflies of the World underwear. It was not a pretty sight, and on seeing this sign he was shaking so much that the vibrations were travelling down his horse's body and causing the poor thing's horseshoes to come loose. "W-we'd better go round it," he stuttered.

But the forest stretched from one side to the other as far as the eye could see, and there seemed to be no choice but to enter.

It was another hot, sunny day – but inside the Forest of the Undead it was cool, dark and gloomy. The singing of the birds suddenly ceased, and Sir Gadabout and the rest of them felt as though a thousand pairs of eyes were watching their every step. The path twisted and turned until they had no idea where they were or which direction they were going in. The branches on either side seemed to be grabbing at them, trying to stop them from going further – or preventing them from getting away. The wind whispering in the leaves sounded like ghostly voices warning them to escape, if they still could. It was such a spooky place that they kept expecting something to jump out at them round every corner – but nothing did.

"Not so bad, after all," commented Sir Gadabout bravely from inside his own saddlebag, into which he had miraculously managed to squeeze his thin body.

But then night began to fall. Dark shapes and shadows could be seen moving here and there. Strange rustling sounds could be heard above and around them. Whenever they saw something moving, they called out: but no answer ever came.

When it had become almost completely dark, and they could barely make out the path before them, a huge, menacing figure suddenly loomed ahead of them, blocking their way.

"Who goes there?" challenged Sir Gadabout, his teeth chattering like castanets.

The reply was a laugh so evil it virtually made Sir Gadabout's Butterflies of the World underwear unravel. The foul breath from the laugh blew the leaves from the trees, as it echoed and thundered in the stillness of the night.

"*Mothuuuuuurgh!*" cried Sir Gadabout waving his arms out of the top of his saddlebag.

"*I am the Lord of the Undead,*" said the figure. "*Welcome to my realm!*"

9

The Three Deadly Challenges

"You are mine forever!" laughed the Lord of the Undead in his deep, echoey voice. His armour was black, and stained with the marks of an unimaginable passage of time. Where his face should have been inside his helmet was also blackness – except for two red eyes that burned like tiny flames. "While you live, you are surrounded by my knights – the Host of the Undead. And when the time comes for you to die, you will not die, but become Undead like the rest of us and haunt this place for all eternity!"

"I don't like the sound of that very much," Herbert remarked.

"Has he gone, yet?" squeaked a voice from inside Sir Gadabout's saddlebag.

"And because you have dared to enter my domain," continued the terrible figure, "you

must complete the Three Deadly Challenges
..."

"Or what?" Sidney Smith challenged him.

The Lord of the Undead turned his pierc-
ing eyes on Sidney Smith. "Do you realise
who you are talking to, pathetic creature?"

"Well, I didn't think it was my Aunty
Gladys. We aren't doing your stupid challenges."

"Then you will die!"

"But you said we would become Undead
– so how can you kill us?"

"Because … Look, will you stop asking
awkward questions? People normally just go

along with what I say — I'm highly terrifying, you know!"

"You look like an overgrown scarecrow to me, mate. The way I see it, we're doomed anyway — so we aren't doing even *one* Deadly Challenge!"

"Oh, *please*! It's so boring, living in here forever. This is the only fun I have!"

"No."

"*Pretty please!*"

"No!"

"Look, I'll make the Three Deadly Challenges easier. Much easier."

"Such as?"

"Find me … oh, something green, something pretty, and a wild animal of some kind."

Sidney Smith thought for a moment. "Okay — you close your eyes and count to a hundred, and we'll go and do it."

"Now wait a minute …" began the Lord of the Undead.

"I bet you can't count to a hundred!" Sidney Smith chided him.

"I jolly well can! I can count to a *thousand*!"

"Well, do it then."

"I will too!"

And with that, the Lord of the Undead closed his eyes and began to count.

"*Let's go, boys!*" whispered Sidney Smith urgently.

They all hurried past the fiend and soon left him far behind.

"Stop!" yelled Sir Gadabout after a few minutes.

"What?" Sidney Smith exclaimed.

"Just there – I saw something pretty!"

"We're not actually *doing* the challenge, sire," Herbert explained.

"But he'll be very disappointed ..."

"As long as we stop messing about, we won't be around when he finds out," said

Sidney Smith. "Quick – he must be up to around six hundred already!"

They raced along the forest path as fast as they could in the darkness, stumbling on the uneven ground, branches lashing their faces. It wasn't long before they heard much terrible wailing and gnashing of teeth behind them: the Lord of the Undead and his many minions were in pursuit, thirsting for revenge at having been tricked.

For a while, no matter how fast they went they could hear the dreadful wailing and gnashing getting ever closer. But eventually Sir Gadabout's own pitiful wailing drowned everything else out, and they couldn't tell how quickly the Lord of the Undead was gaining on them.

Soon, they didn't have to listen for their pursuers – a glance over their shoulders revealed hundreds of ghostly figures rushing towards them.

"Keep going," cried Sidney Smith, who had by far the sharpest eyes. "I can see the edge of the forest!"

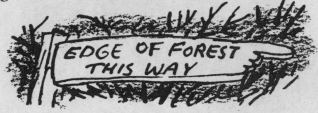

Now, Sir Gadabout stopped wailing, and like a prayer began to repeat, "*They can't come out of the forest … they can't come out of the forest …*" over and over again.

At long last they burst from the canopy of trees into open fields. Sir Gadabout looked back.

"*They're coming out of the forest! AAAAAAAAAARGH!*"

Not even the Undead had heard a scream like the one emitted by Sir Gadabout, and the whole horde came to an awestruck halt, wondering what manner of strange creature

they were actually chasing. This allowed Sir Gadabout and Co. to escape at last.

Once it seemed they were clear of danger, at least for the time being, they all turned to little Roger.

"This was all your doing – *again!*" Herbert accused.

"I never!"

"I shall tell King Arthur, who will tell your father," added Sir Gadabout.

Seeing that he was on very thin ice, Roger showed his true colours. "A lot of good that will do!" he said, laughing at them all. "My father will believe *me*. Everyone always believes me – and I'll tell them it was all *your* fault!" And he ended with a laugh that sounded even nastier than that of the Lord of the Undead.

Worse still, Sir Gadabout had a horrible feeling that Roger was probably right. If he could make a great knight like himself believe his stories, what chance did anyone else stand? "We're all doomed! Finished!" he moaned.

"Worry not, Sir Madabout," whispered Sidney Smith, hopping into Sir Gadabout's lap. "I've got a plan …"

10

King Alf and Queen Pete

On the morning that they came in sight of Camelot at long last, Sidney Smith rose very early while the rest of them were asleep, and hurried the last few miles to the castle on his own, unnoticed by any of the others ...

By the time Sir Gadabout, Herbert and Roger arrived at Camelot, the main gates were wide open, and two figures were there waiting to greet them. They were actually Alf, the castle caretaker, and Pete, his assistant. But Alf was wearing his poshest clothes and a crown made out of tin painted gold. Pete was wearing a dress and a wig of long blonde hair.

Sidney Smith strode forward. "Pray bow before their majesties, King Arthur and Queen Guinevere!" he commanded.

"But that's —"

Just before Sir Gadabout could give the

game away, Herbert did something he had never done to his master in his whole life. He kicked him in the shins.

"*Oww!*"

"Sorry, sire – I tripped. I think we'd better bow."

When the bowing was over, Roger sprang forward and blinked his big, tearful blue eyes. "Your majesties, terrible things have been happening to me – and it's all *their* fault! I'm actually just a poor servant boy who they kidnapped, and then they –"

"We know what has happened," said King Arthur — sorry — *Alf*.

"I'm glad because after they kidnapped me they made me go to this castle and ..."

"We know that you are a Little Horror, and not to be trusted!" added Guinevere — sorry — *Pete*.

Roger now turned his eyes on Sidney Smith. "You mean you'd rather believe a mangy moggy than me, the son of the most powerful knight in the North?"

"Ah! So you *aren't* a poor servant boy!" cried King Alf — sorry — well, you know what I mean by now.

Realising the game was up, Roger stamped past them into Camelot itself. "Wait till my father arrives with his army, you pathetic lot! *He'll* believe me, and then you'll pay for this!"

And he began to stamp around the castle grounds, crying at the top of his voice, "KING ARTHUR IS A STUPID BIG-NOSE!!! GUINEVERE IS AN UGLY OLD FISH-FACE!!!"

"I haven't got a big nose!" Alf complained (but unfortunately, he had).

"I'm not old!" added Pete (which was true).

And as the *real* King Arthur and Queen
Guinevere came out to welcome the trav-
ellers home, Roger was parading past them
yelling, "KING ARTHUR'S GOT A
BRAIN THE SIZE OF AN APPLE
PIP! SMELLY GUINEVERE NEVER
CHANGES HER UNDERWEAR!"

Alf muttered, "It would have to be a big
apple, that's all I can say."

Pete kept quiet.

"Now, now," warned the real King Arthur.
"What's all this about?"

In reply, Roger stamped on the king's foot,
and bit Guinevere's knee. He was promptly

arrested by the guards as he tried to run away.

Alf and Pete were most relieved to get back to their ordinary jobs. They had never realised how stressful being royal could be.

After Sir Gadabout's untimely return, the real king and queen, and most of the rest of Camelot, had been talking about nothing else than the fate of Gads and Co. On discovering what Sir Gadabout and his friends had had to put up with on their long journey, and knowing that Sir Lancelot would soon be able to knock Roger into shape, they threw a little party for them that evening.

"You should have seen the look I gave Lord Stonefist," said Herbert, trying to make himself heard above the hubub of the party. "I could tell he didn't want to tangle with *me!*"

"Of course," said Sir Gadabout, "I had my suspicions about that Little Horror right from the very beginning. I didn't say anything so as not to worry the others."

"Yeah, and I just saw a pig go flying by," said Sidney Smith.

Sir Gadabout looked up. "Ooh – missed it!"

There was still the small matter of the three most powerful armies in the land marching on Camelot. Guinevere dealt with Sir Dexter and Sir Sinistral — she had a way of talking to men. They all went away trying to fit together a variety of fascinating wooden puzzles she had made. (These were actually meant for their children — but the grown-ups had to try them out, you understand.)

Sir Pelligrew the Portly arrived with his men, still thinking that Roger had been kidnapped – but after seeing the armies of the Left and Right off, Guinevere was able to persuade him of the truth about the Little Horror, and she sent him on his way after telling him the one about the vicar and the cheeky monkey, and he laughed so much all the way back that the weatherman spoke of hurricanes over most of Yorkshire that day.

Lord Stonefist was a different matter. He had the strongest army of all, and he was angrier than ever. *But* it turned out that he had realised how peaceful life was without Roger. Odd things had stopped happening. Unexplained wars had stopped breaking out. Loud and rude noises at the breakfast table had ceased. So when it was learned that Lord Stonefist had come only because he had heard a rumour that Roger was to be *returned* to him, he was easily satisfied. In fact, Lord Stonefist was so relieved to hear that Roger was staying at Camelot for a number of years that it *seemed* he shed a tear of joy – but Ernie said it was merely an eyelash stuck in his eye.

The invading Host of the Undead presented a trickier proposition. Merlin had to sort

them out with an Unspell, which whisked them straight back to their forest where they Unlived ever after.

And Sir Percy was almost able to sit down again.

So although everyone knew deep down that Sir Gadabout was still the Worst Knight in the World, it was quite a long time after the party before they mentioned it again.

Also by Martyn Beardsley

Sir Gadabout

When the fair Guinevere goes missing, Sir Gadabout sets out on a quest to rescue her . . . and he's in for some catastrophic adventures!

Sir Gadabout Gets Worse

When Excalibur is stolen, Gads sets off with his trusty band of followers to find the evil Sir Rudyard the Rancid. They must face the worst if they are to return the mighty sword to its rightful home.

Sir Gadabout and The Ghost

When he sees the ghost of Sir Henry Hirsute, Gads runs up the wall in fright. But soon he's off on another calamitous quest – to clear Sir Henry's name of the ghastly crime of pilchard-stealing.

Sir Gadabout Does His Best

Take a three legged goat, a hungry dragon and a bad tempered, short knight called Sir Mistabit. Mix well with Sir Gadabout, the worst knight in the world, and his trusty companions.

What have you got? A recipe for disaster as Sir Gadabout and co. set off on a chaotic and hilarious brand new adventure.